Paying College Athletes

Gail Terp

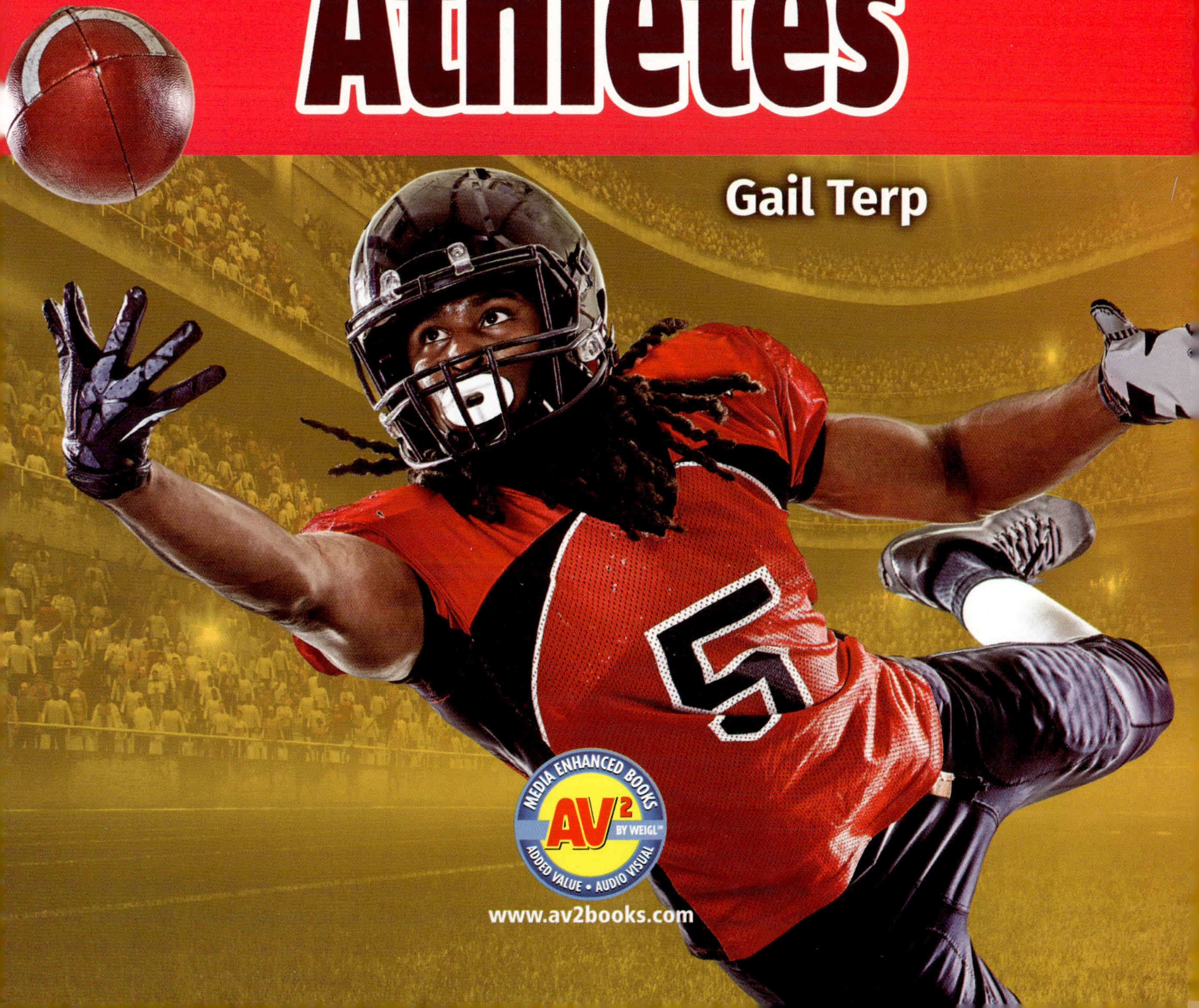

AV² BY WEIGL
MEDIA ENHANCED BOOKS
ADDED VALUE • AUDIO VISUAL

www.av2books.com

Go to **www.av2books.com**, and enter this book's unique code.

BOOK CODE

AVM84864

AV² by Weigl brings you media enhanced books that support active learning.

AV² provides enriched content that supplements and complements this book. Weigl's AV² books strive to create inspired learning and engage young minds in a total learning experience.

Your AV² Media Enhanced books come alive with...

Audio
Listen to sections of the book read aloud.

Key Words
Study vocabulary, and complete a matching word activity.

Video
Watch informative video clips.

Quizzes
Test your knowledge.

Embedded Weblinks
Gain additional information for research.

Slide Show
View images and captions, and prepare a presentation.

Try This!
Complete activities and hands-on experiments.

... and much, much more!

Published by AV² by Weigl
350 5th Avenue, 59th Floor
New York, NY 10118
Website: www.av2books.com

Copyright © 2020 AV² by Weigl
All rights reserved. No part of this publication may be reproduced, stored in a retrieval system, or transmitted in any form or by any means, electronic, mechanical, photocopying, recording, or otherwise, without the prior written permission of the publisher.

Library of Congress Cataloging-in-Publication Data

Names: Terp, Gail, 1951- author.
Title: Paying college athletes / Gail Terp.
Description: New York : AV2 by Weigl, [2020] | Series: Debating the issues | Includes index. | Audience: Grade 7 to 8.
Identifiers: LCCN 2018051722 (print) | LCCN 2018058292 (ebook) | ISBN 9781489696069 (Multi User ebook) | ISBN 9781489696076 (Single User ebook) | ISBN 9781489696045 (hardcover : alk. paper) | ISBN 9781489696052 (softcover : alk. paper)
Subjects: LCSH: College sports--Economic aspects--United States--Juvenile literature. | College athletes--United States--Economic conditions--Juvenile literature.
Classification: LCC GV351 (ebook) | LCC GV351 .T42 2019 (print) | DDC 796.04/3--dc23
LC record available at https://lccn.loc.gov/2018051722

Printed in Guangzhou, China
1 2 3 4 5 6 7 8 9 0 23 22 21 20 19

022019
112318

First published by North Star in 2018

Project Coordinator: Ryan Smith Designer: Ana María Vidal

Every reasonable effort has been made to trace ownership and to obtain permission to reprint copyright material. The publishers would be pleased to have any errors or omissions brought to their attention so that they may be corrected in subsequent printings.

Weigl acknowledges Getty Images, iStock, and Alamy as its primary image suppliers for this title.

Paying College Athletes

Contents

In 2015, 47 percent of people in the United States followed college sports.

An Introduction to College Athletics

In many colleges, sports play an important role in the life of the school. Some top division college teams become famous. Students, parents, and other community members buy tickets to games and cheer for their teams. TV stations broadcast the games for fans at home. Sporting goods companies supply the players' equipment. This is a good way to advertise their brands. The top teams bring in huge amounts of money. Each year, college sports earn hundreds of millions of dollars for their schools.

Student athletes are the reason colleges take in all this money. If athletes did not play, there would be no ticket sales. TV stations would have no college games to broadcast. Currently, many college athletes receive free **tuition**, but they do not share in the money that their colleges earn from the games. This has led to a heated debate. Should college athletes be paid for playing? Some people believe it is only fair that student athletes receive a share of the money they helped generate. Others think paying college athletes would interfere with the athletes' schooling.

Many groups are involved in this debate, including athletes, coaches, and colleges. Owners of TV stations and sporting goods companies have opinions, too. Another group involved in the debate is the National Collegiate Athletic Association (NCAA). The NCAA is the organization in charge of college sports in the United States. It writes and enforces the rules for each sport.

The issue of paying college athletes is complex. Stakes are high for all who are involved. Both sides have strong arguments for their views.

For many colleges, sports games serve as large social events.

Timeline

1906 The NCAA is formed as the Intercollegiate Athletic Association of the United States.

1939 Freshman players at the University of Pittsburgh go on strike to demand equal compensation with senior players.

1948 The NCAA introduces a "Sanity Code" that restricts financial aid for athletes to school expenses such as tuition.

1955 The term "student-athlete" is first used as a legal defense against those seeking compensation for sport-related injuries.

1973 The NCAA prohibits schools from offering multi-year scholarships. The schools get to decide if they want to renew these yearly scholarships with their athletes.

2018 An FBI investigation reveals several coaches, sports agents, and sponsor employees broke NCAA rules and provided extra financial incentives to entice athletic prospects to join their teams.

PRO

Florida State University Seminoles football season tickets cost $330–$850.

Athletes Deserve a Portion of the Money They Generate

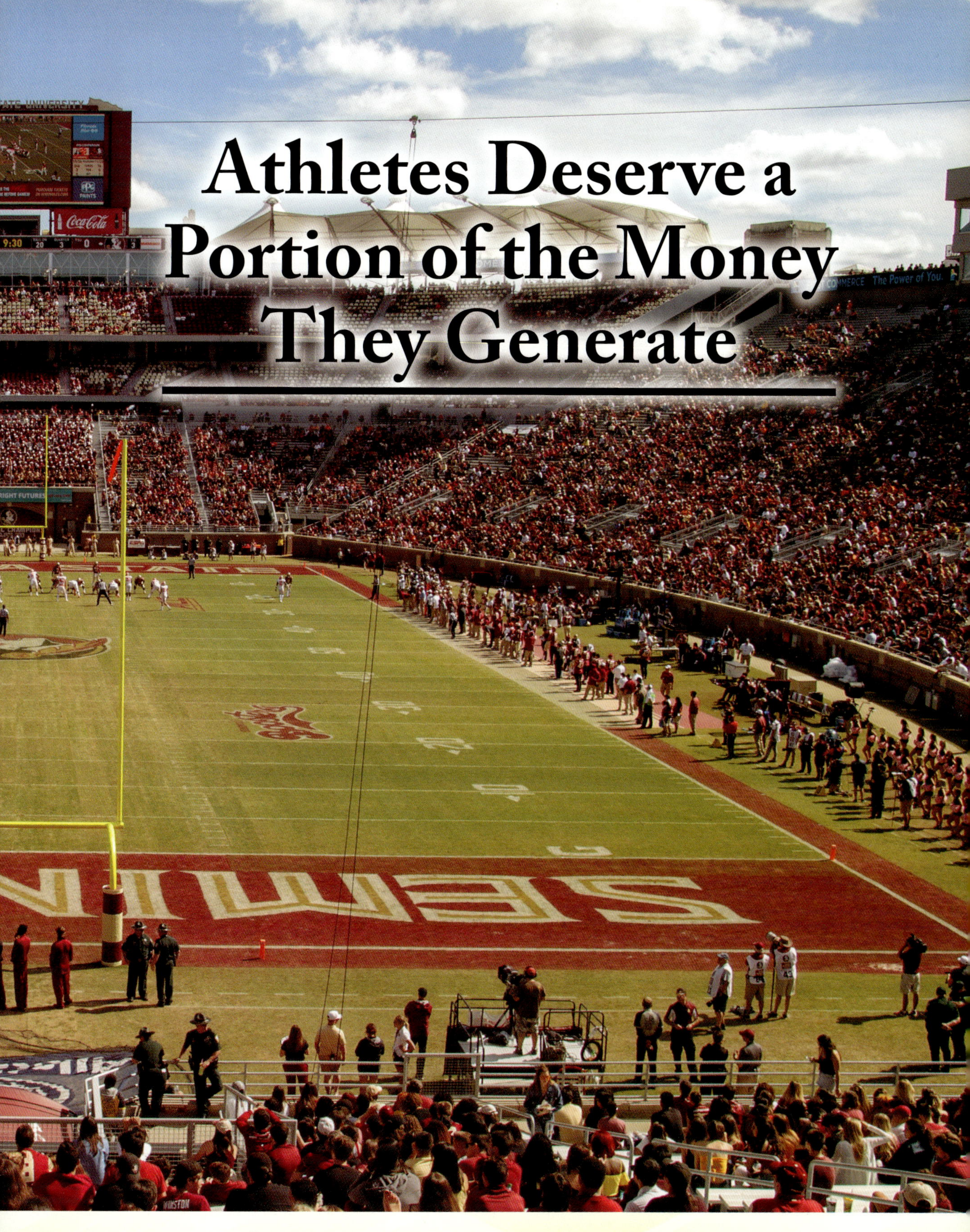

The money that athletes generate for their colleges comes from several sources. Ticket sales for games bring in money. Fans also buy **merchandise**, such as team shirts and other products with team names and logos on them. In addition, **alumni** donate money to the sports programs of the colleges they once attended.

TV stations pay colleges large sums of money to broadcast games. One example is basketball. In 2016, a TV network agreed to pay the NCAA $8.8 billion dollars for the right to broadcast the men's basketball tournament from 2024 to 2032.

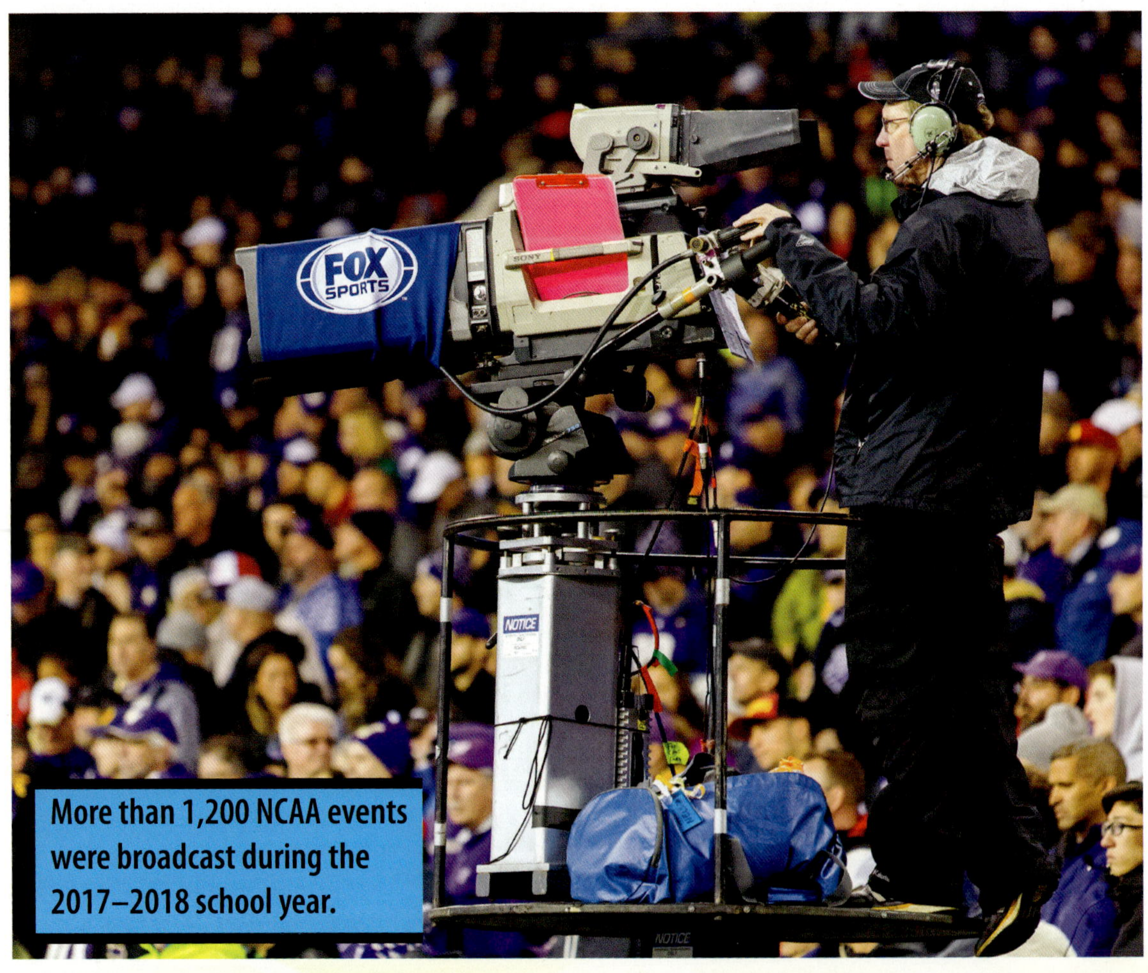

More than 1,200 NCAA events were broadcast during the 2017–2018 school year.

NCAA rules determine how an athlete's name, photo, or likeness can be used. The schools may use them in advertisements and on merchandise. Schools may hang posters with athletes' names and pictures to advertise upcoming games. They may also sell jerseys for their teams' top players. Some schools even sell players' likenesses to companies that make video games. Any profits from the sale of these products go to the NCAA or to the respective schools. NCAA rules ban student athletes from profiting from any of these sales.

DID YOU KNOW?

Coaches earn a portion of the money that their programs receive. In 2016, the top five coaches in college sports earned between $6 million and $9 million.

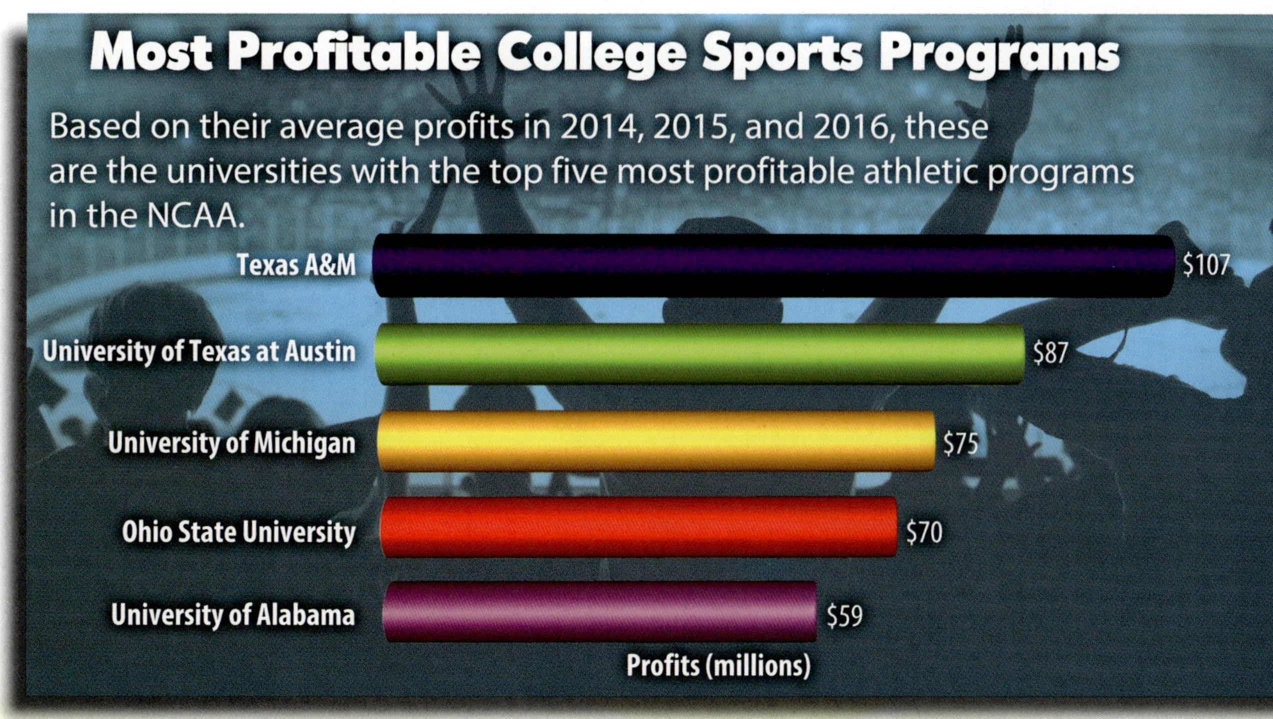

Advocates for paying college athletes believe athletes should share in the wealth they generate for their schools. After all, it is the athletes' performance on the field that creates profit opportunities. Therefore, the athletes should earn more than only their scholarships.

However, not everyone agrees on the best method for paying athletes. Some suggest that colleges pay each athlete a minimum salary, such as $25,000 per year. Another idea is to let athletes earn money for each game they play.

Some college athletes may take time before or after an event to sign autographs.

Some people believe athletes should receive a share of the money their names, photos, and likenesses earn. For instance, if a video game uses a basketball player's likeness, the athlete should share in the game's profits. If football players sign autographs at a sporting goods store, they should be allowed to accept pay from the store's owner.

Not all advocates agree on how athletes should be paid, but they do agree that receiving payment is fair. Discussions will continue regarding the best way to make fair payments.

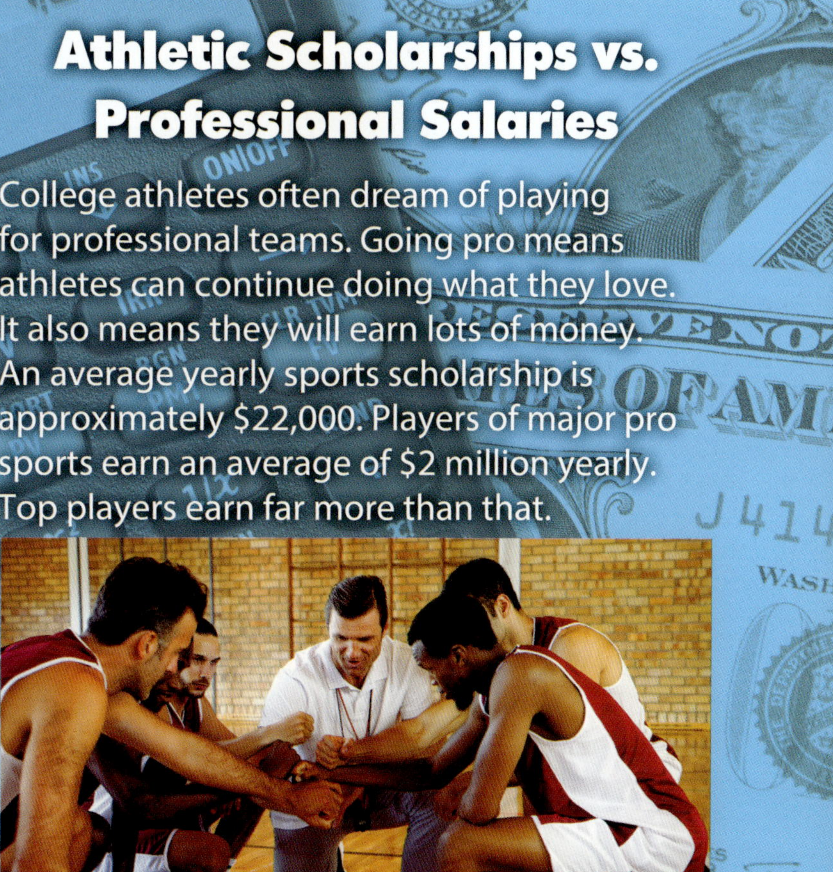

Athletic Scholarships vs. Professional Salaries

College athletes often dream of playing for professional teams. Going pro means athletes can continue doing what they love. It also means they will earn lots of money. An average yearly sports scholarship is approximately $22,000. Players of major pro sports earn an average of $2 million yearly. Top players earn far more than that.

College athletes often lack the time and energy for studying.

Long-Term Scholarships Support an Athlete's Education

College athletes spend long hours involved in their sports. NCAA rules state that practice sessions should take no more than 20 hours each week. However, practice sessions are not athletes' only sports-related activities. Athletes often have lengthy trips traveling to and from games. Coaches have them watch video of practice sessions, looking for ways to improve. They take part in workouts, attend team meetings, and compete in games. These time commitments can add up to more than 40 hours per week.

Game days count as three hours of an athlete's week, but this does not include travel time and meetings.

Advocates for pay think student athletes should be paid for their hard work. However, salaries are not the only options for payment. Many advocates think colleges should pay athletes through educational support. This support would come in the form of long-term tuition payments.

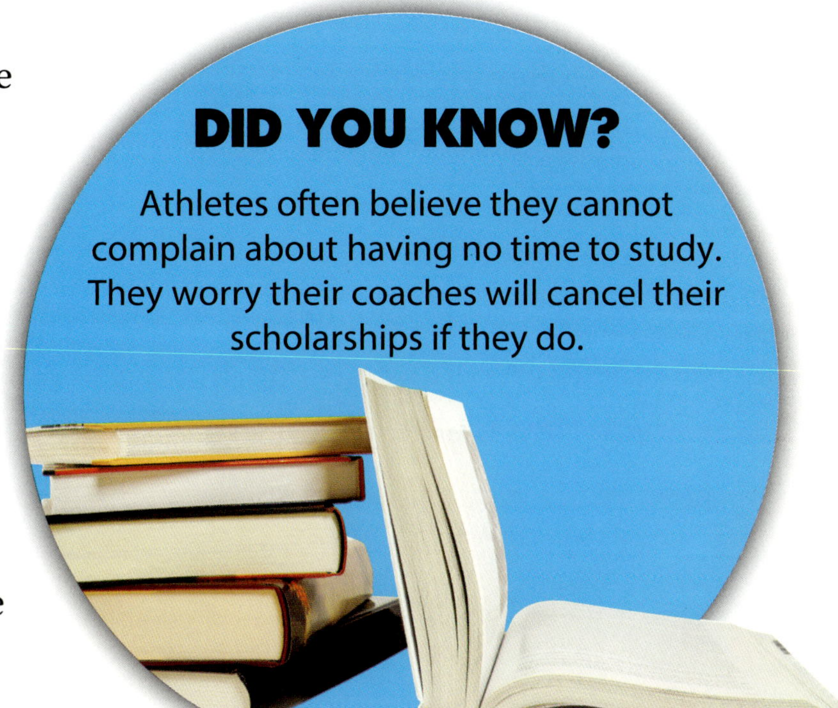

Sports often leave student athletes with little time for academics. In the time they have left for classwork, athletes are often too tired to do their best. Student athletes who do not maintain strong grades may lose their scholarships.

Many schools offer tutoring to student athletes. However, this support is not always enough. Some schools take other steps to improve athletes' grades. Athletes are encouraged to take easy classes. Schools may arrange for others to do athletes' assignments. Unlike tutoring, these actions do not help athletes learn. When caught, schools receive fines and other punishments.

Many colleges attempt to support athletes' educations through one-year scholarships. However, these scholarships pose problems. One-year scholarships must be renewed each year. Coaches can choose not to renew them if an athlete is not performing as well as they would like. If athletes' coaches decide to cancel their scholarships, the athletes must pay their own tuition. Many athletes cannot afford the cost of tuition. This makes attending college impossible.

Coaches and athletes agree that there needs to be a balance between sport and school.

In contrast, multiyear scholarships can last for two to five years. These scholarships continue even if the athlete is no longer able to play. However, multiyear scholarships are uncommon. Most colleges only offer one-year scholarships to student athletes.

Many advocates for pay think athletes should be paid through long-term scholarships. They propose eliminating one-year scholarships, and they want all athletic scholarships guaranteed for at least four years. That way, athletes do not have to worry about paying for their schooling.

Some advocates think scholarships alone are not enough. They want a system that helps student athletes manage their workloads. This system would allow athletes to take fewer classes each term. Their scholarships would then be extended for up to eight years. This would enable hard-working athletes to earn their degrees.

PRO

Payment of Medical Costs Helps Athletes Recover from Injury

The overall cost of injuries in contact college sports ranges from $446 million to $1.5 billion a year.

Practice sessions can be long and punishing for college athletes. Preseason practices start weeks before the first games of the season. For some sports, practice begins in the heat of summer. Players work on skills and weight train for strength. They play practice games. When the official season begins, players practice less. Although fewer in number, these sessions are still intense.

Injuries can happen during practice sessions, warm-ups, or games.

Practice is important for preparing athletes for competition. However, practice sessions can also lead to injuries. Advocates for paying college athletes believe colleges, or the NCAA, should pay for athletes' medical costs. These payments would help injured athletes receive the treatment they need.

Some athletic injuries are minor and involve a short recovery time. Others are more serious and require long recovery times. For example, some athletes injure their anterior cruciate ligament (ACL). This injury affects the knee and often requires surgery. Recovery from an ACL injury takes many months before an athlete is able to play again.

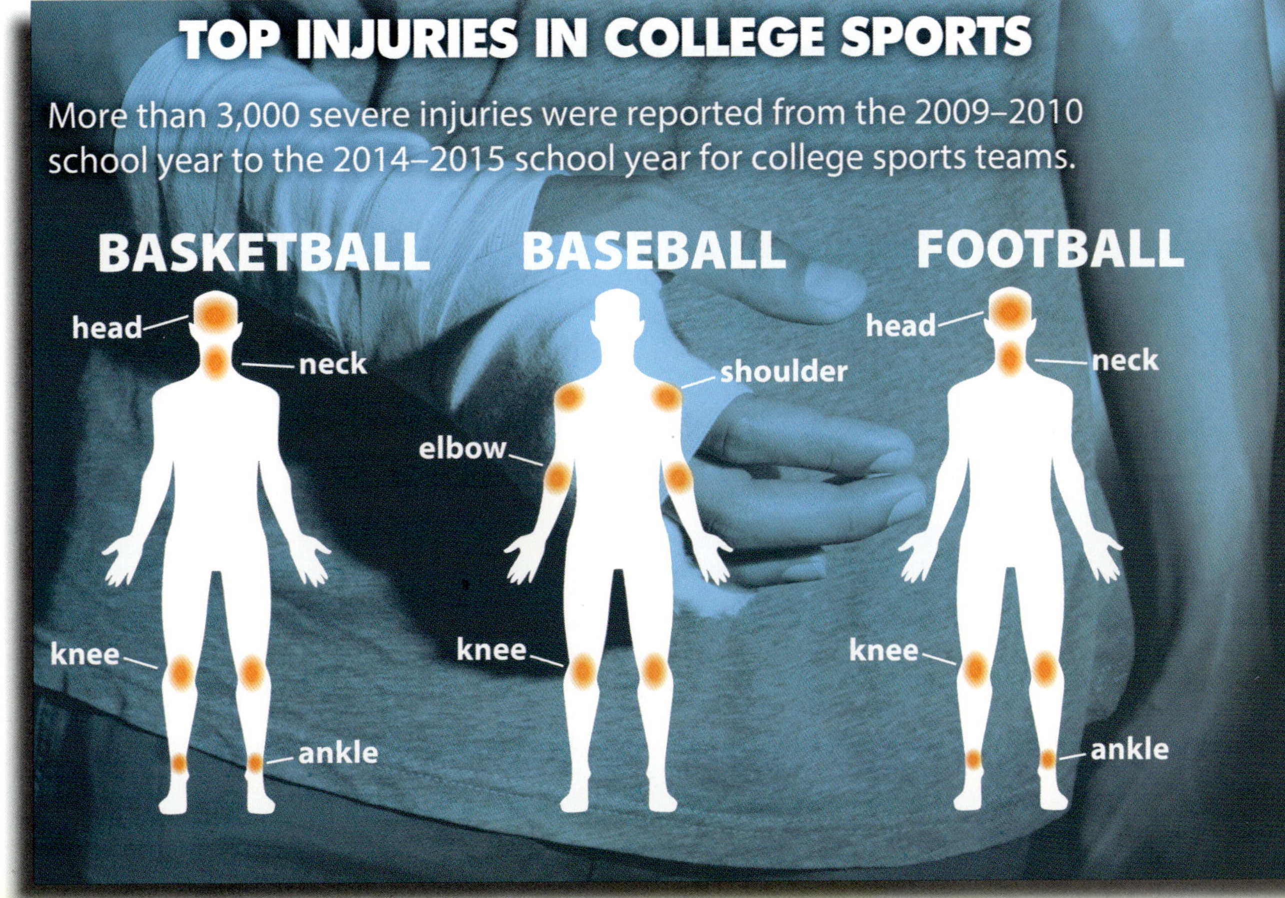

A concussion is a type of brain injury caused by a hard blow to the head. It is among the most serious injuries athletes face. Concussions cause many **symptoms**, including headaches, nausea, and depression. When an athlete has had several concussions, the symptoms can be long lasting.

To play on a college team, athletes must carry medical **insurance** that covers athletic injuries. Unfortunately, this insurance does not always cover all expenses. As a result, the families of injured athletes may have high medical bills.

Long-term injuries can create a heavy financial burden on families. Recovery from concussions and other injuries can take years. In some cases, injuries may affect players for the rest of their lives. Some colleges provide financial help for long-term injuries. However, most do not.

College football players are seven times more likely to be injured in a game than in practice.

Many former student athletes have brought **lawsuits** against their colleges and the NCAA. These athletes suffer from the long-term effects of concussions. They claim their schools did not protect them from the dangers of concussions. The courts have to decide whether these athletes should receive money for their medical costs.

Advocates for pay want colleges, or the NCAA, to pay for athletes' medical insurance. This insurance would cover all sports injuries.

If an athlete gets injured during any sports activity, insurance would pay for the athlete's full treatment. It would also cover the long-term effects from injuries for as long as they continue.

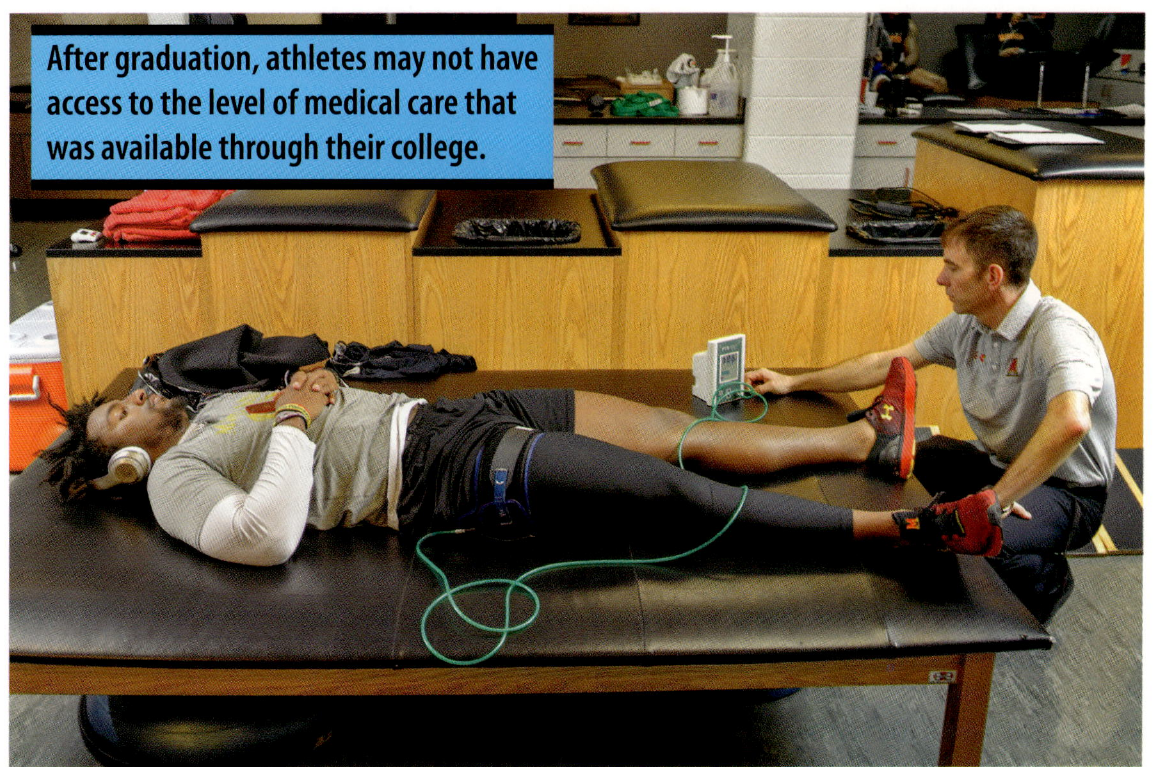

After graduation, athletes may not have access to the level of medical care that was available through their college.

CON

College athletes can receive extra financial aid in order to help cover the cost of materials such as textbooks.

Athletes Are Already Paid through Scholarships and Benefits

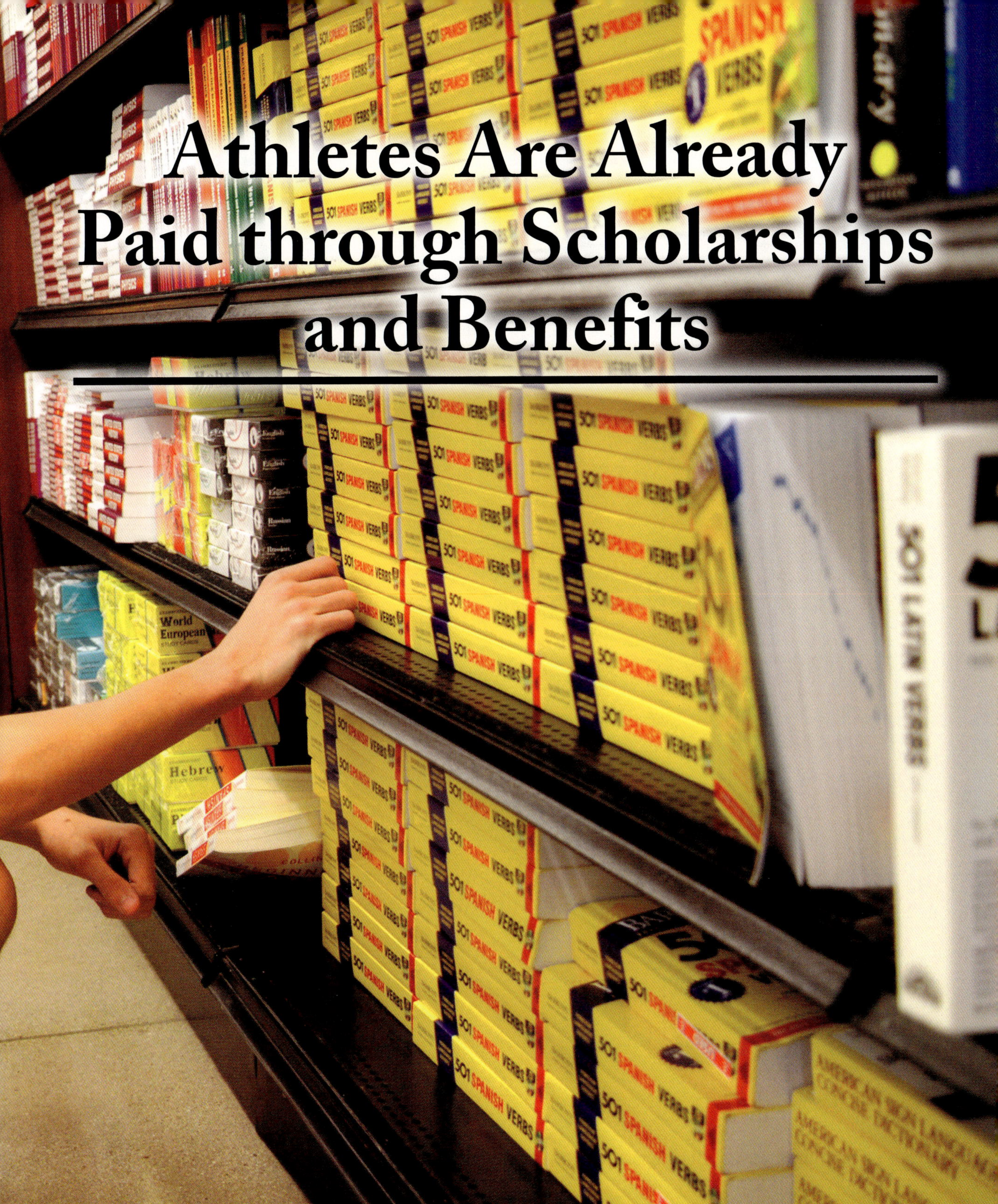

Colorado State University's state-of-the-art weight room was part of a $20 million renovation.

Opponents of paying college athletes believe short-term scholarships are payment enough. College programs in at least 35 sports offer scholarships to student athletes. Scholarship sports include archery, baseball, golf, soccer, tennis, and many more. In 2016, the highest one-year men's scholarship was in basketball. The player received $53,075. For women's scholarships in 2016, the highest was in gymnastics for $63,337. However, most scholarships are not that high. The average is between $10,000 and $30,000.

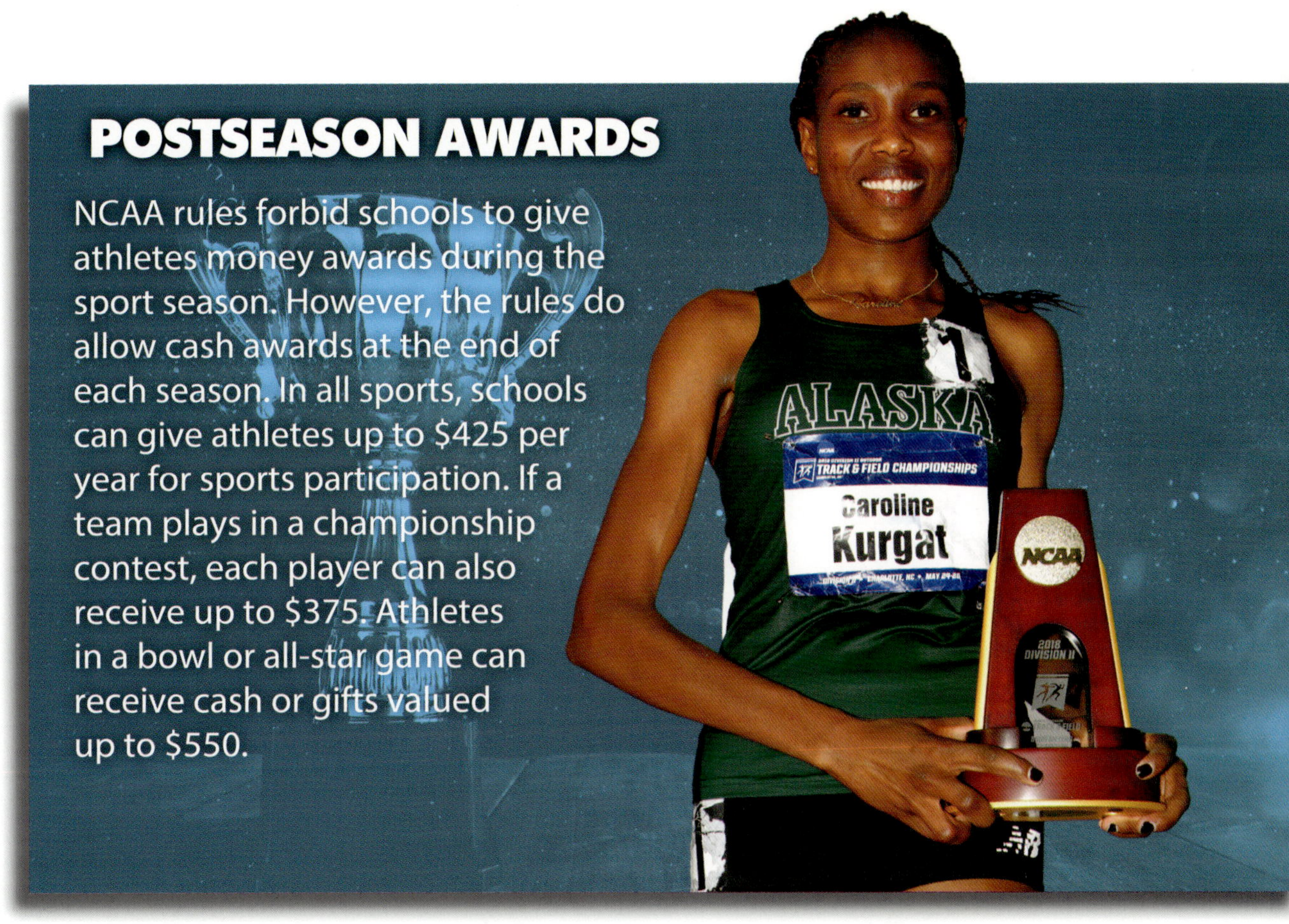

POSTSEASON AWARDS

NCAA rules forbid schools to give athletes money awards during the sport season. However, the rules do allow cash awards at the end of each season. In all sports, schools can give athletes up to $425 per year for sports participation. If a team plays in a championship contest, each player can also receive up to $375. Athletes in a bowl or all-star game can receive cash or gifts valued up to $550.

Most of the scholarship money a student receives pays for tuition, plus **room and board**. Scholarships also usually pay for students' books. These can be expensive. Recently, NCAA rules permitted colleges to offer athletes a **stipend**. Athletes can use stipends to pay for school expenses that their scholarships do not cover. Stipends are typically $3,000 to $7,000 per year.

Most college students have high debts when they graduate. The average debt for a college graduate in 2017 was approximately $27,000. It can take students years to pay this money back. Therefore, athletic scholarships give athletes a financial advantage over many other students. Some college athletes who have scholarships graduate with no student debt.

College athletes receive many benefits in addition to scholarships. For instance, they get to work with top coaches and learn skills in their sports. They also train in state-of-the-art facilities. Football teams often have huge indoor practice fields and sports buildings containing first-class weight rooms. There are **hydrotherapy** rooms to treat sore muscles and injuries and rooms for athletes to relax in, many of which have high-end video systems. These sports facilities are only for student athletes. Some schools and coaches think these benefits work as substitutes for athlete pay.

College athletes attending Howard University have the opportunity to visit the Howard University Gallery of Art.

An opportunity to attend college offers more than academic benefits. College campus life is rich with many opportunities. Students can go to museums and engage in other art experiences. They can attend concerts, dances, and theater performances. Many athletes also become involved in the community. Some volunteer in schools near their college. Others raise funds for people in need. These campus opportunities offer college athletes valuable experiences and worthwhile skills.

CON

While most college athletes strive to succeed in both athletics and academics, one is often prioritized over the other.

Payments Put the Focus on Athletics over Academics

The NCAA values the importance of graduation for all student athletes. To compete, athletes must meet certain academic standards each year. They must take a required number of courses each semester and maintain passing grades. Student athletes who do not meet these requirements are not eligible for competition.

College students need to earn an average of 15 credits a semester in order to graduate in four years.

Some people worry that paying college athletes would draw athletes' focus away from academics. College athletes are supposed to focus on being a student first and an athlete second. Very few student athletes go on to play professional sports, but student athletes who graduate gain many benefits in the job market.

Professional athletes are paid to win games. Paying college athletes would place pressure on them to perform like professionals. Student athletes might think that winning is the top priority. They may start taking sports more seriously than school. Without a firm focus on academics, most students would never graduate.

GOING PRO

The 2017 percentages of NCAA student athletes that go on to play for a major professional team reflects the general trend of professional sport opportunities for student athletes.

Sport	NCAA Participants	Percentage Who Go Professional
Men's Baseball	34,554	9.1%
Men's Hockey	4,102	5.6%
Men's Football	73,660	1.5%
Men's Soccer	24,803	1.4%
Men's Basketball	18,684	1.1%
Women's Basketball	16,593	0.9%

Nicole Mann was a member of the 2013 class of NASA astronauts.

Student athletes have job advantages when they graduate from college. College graduates tend to earn more and have better health benefits. Also, they are less likely to be unemployed. In addition, many employers like to hire former college athletes. Companies want employees who are team players. They look for individuals who can work toward goals and persevere through failure. Employers also want workers who know how to manage their time. Athletes typically have all these skills.

Many former athletes credit sports for their success after school. For example, Tom Catena played football in college before becoming a doctor. As a student athlete, Catena learned time-management and teamwork skills. Another example is astronaut Nicole Mann, who played soccer in college. College sports taught Mann how to balance multiple responsibilities. They also taught her to focus.

College Athlete Graduation Rates

The NCAA keeps track of graduation rates for college athletes. According to the NCAA's Graduation Success Rate (GSR) scale, graduation rates have increased since 2002. The 2002 graduation rate for student athletes was 74 percent. The 2018 rate had increased to 88 percent. The GSR is used only for student athletes. It cannot be compared with the nonathlete student graduation rate.

College sports are not about money. Students should be able to focus on more than winning. As college athletes, they have the unique opportunity to build skills for the future. Playing for money, or simply to win, takes away the true spirit of sports. It also fails to prepare students for their future.

The social skills learned from playing sports, such as accountability and taking criticism, help student athletes when they enter the workforce.

The Harvard athletics program costs the school more than it earns. Only one-third of their football stadium was filled during the 2017–2018 season.

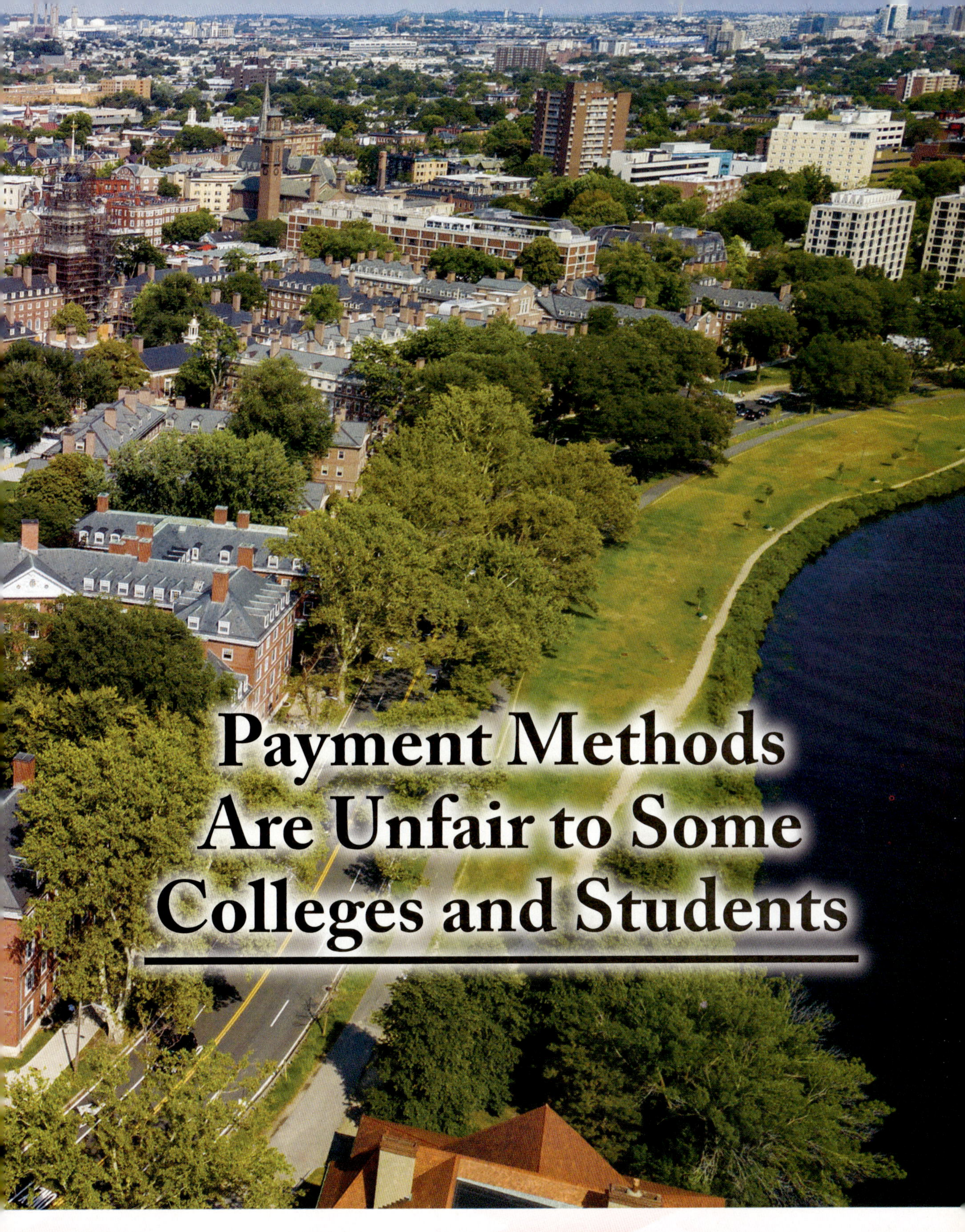

Payment Methods Are Unfair to Some Colleges and Students

Some colleges earn lots of money from their sports programs. They use the money to pay for training facilities, coaches, and general college expenses. These schools could probably afford to pay their athletes. However, athlete salaries would take funds away from other important uses.

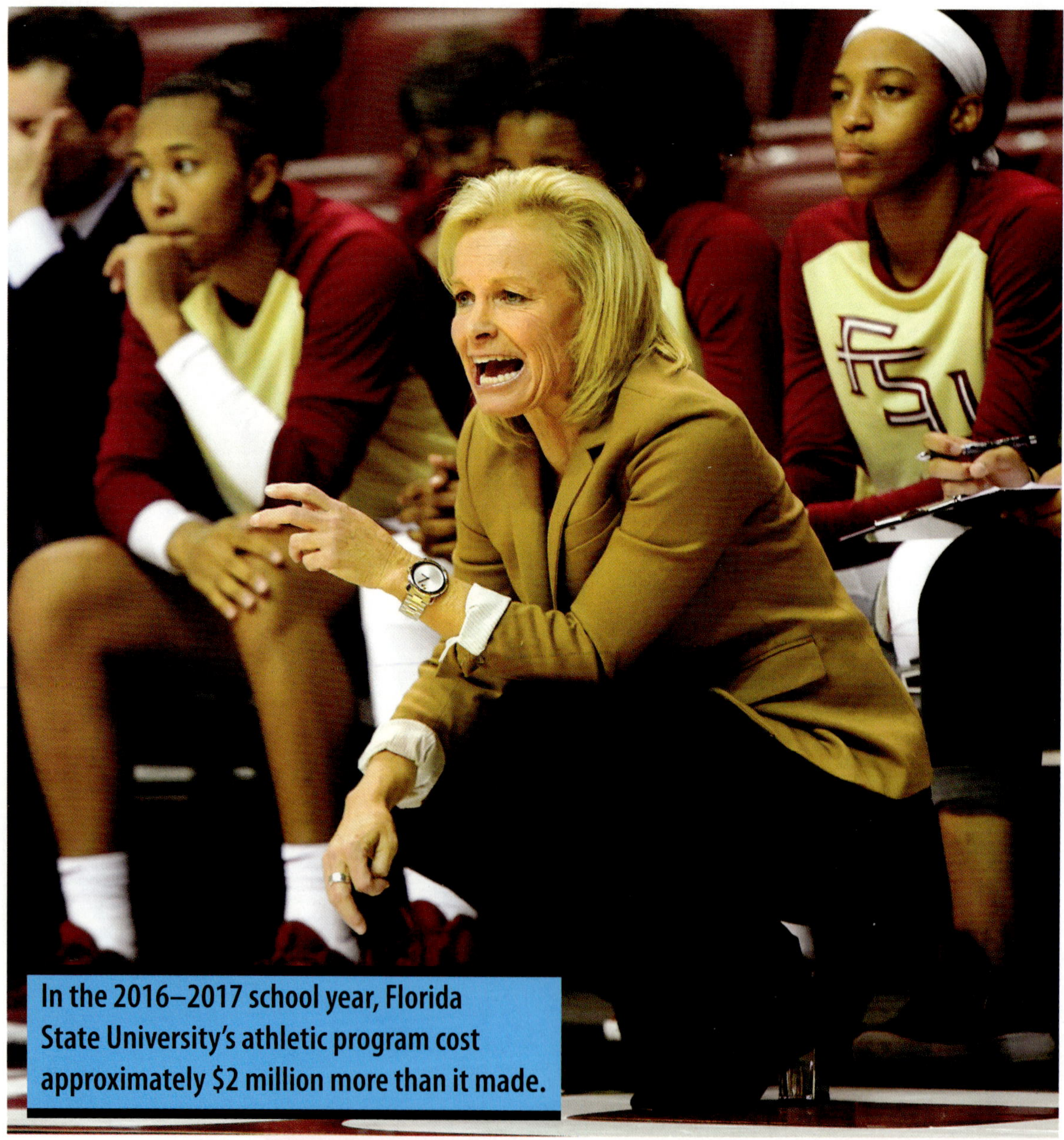
In the 2016–2017 school year, Florida State University's athletic program cost approximately $2 million more than it made.

Most colleges do not earn money from their sports. These colleges maintain sports programs with money from their general college budgets. If schools were forced to pay their athletes, other items in their budgets would suffer. Some schools might have to raise tuition rates and give fewer scholarships. Should paying athletes become too difficult, some schools might do away with sports altogether.

A college golf program can cost five times the amount of money it generates.

If the NCAA allows colleges to pay student athletes, colleges must decide which athletes should receive a salary. They could decide to pay every athlete. However, some sports do not earn money for schools. Athletes of sports that do make a profit, such as football and basketball, may think this is unfair. After all, it is their sport that earns the school money. Colleges could decide to pay only football and basketball players, but athletes of other sports might think this is unfair. These athletes also work hard and put in long hours. Finding a payment method that is fair to all athletes would be difficult.

DID YOU KNOW?

The majority of Division I college sports programs lose money for their schools.

Nonathlete students may also think paying student athletes is unfair. Most colleges charge students an athletics fee. Colleges use this fee to support their athletic programs. Athletic fees can be several hundred dollars per year. Many students have complained about paying this fee. They may be more upset if their money is used to pay student athletes.

If colleges decide to pay athletes, other issues of fairness would arise. Schools would have to determine how much to pay athletes. They could pay all athletes the same amount, or they could base athletes' pay on the number of games they play. Salaries could even be based on athletes' grades.

Each payment method creates its own problem. For example, one option is to base athletes' pay on the amount of money they earn for the school. Colleges with top teams could offer athletes as much as they wanted. Top athletes would choose the school that would pay them the most. This would give schools with more resources an unfair advantage. Schools with fewer resources would no longer be able to compete.

Pros and Cons Summary

PROS

- College athletes deserve a portion of the money generated through ticket sales.
- Schools should pay athletes when using their faces or names on promotional materials.
- College athletes should be paid for their hard work and long practice sessions.
- Schools should provide more long-term scholarships so athletes have time to graduate.
- Student athletes are at risk of injury every time they play. Colleges should cover all medical costs for treatment of injuries.

CONS

- Student athletes already receive scholarships that cover tuition, room, and board.
- College sports programs offer benefits instead of pay, such as training with top coaches.
- Paying college athletes would draw their focus away from school.
- Paying college athletes would put too much focus on winning and making money.
- If colleges pay athletes, schools might have to raise tuition or cut school programs.
- No payment method would be fair to all colleges and students.

College Sports Map

College sports have become incredibly popular. Spectators from across the country fill stadiums and tune in on television. The 2018 College Football Playoff National Championship was broadcast to approximately 30 million people, and the NCAA Division I Men's Basketball Tournament final game was broadcast to more than 16 million people.

Rose Bowl Stadium – Pasadena, California The Rose Bowl is a college football game held on either New Year's Eve or New Year's Day as a part of Pasadena's Tournament of Roses. In 2018, more than 28 million people tuned in to watch the game on television.

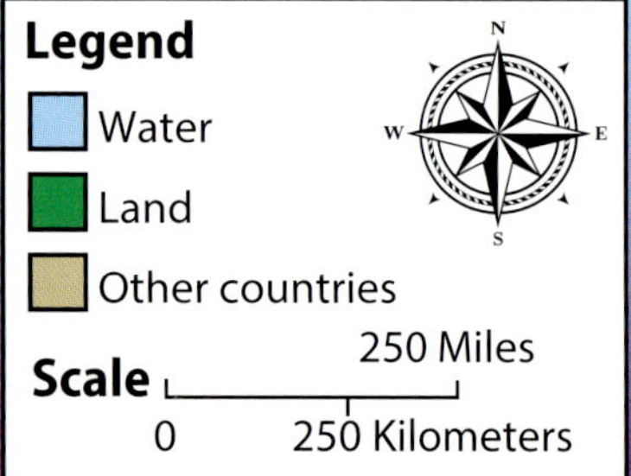

NCAA Headquarters – Indianapolis, Indiana The NCAA moved its headquarters from Kansas City, Kansas, to Indianapolis, Indiana, in 1999. Expansions were completed on the Indianapolis headquarters in 2012.
Madison Square Garden – New York, New York In 1940, the first televised college basketball game was broadcasted from Madison Square Garden. The game featured Fordham University and the University of Pittsburgh.
States
North Dakota
Minnesota
South Dakota
Wisconsin
Michigan
Maine
New York
New Hampshire
Vermont
Massachusetts
Rhode Island
Connecticut
New Jersey
Pennsylvania
Ohio
Indiana
Illinois
Iowa
Nebraska
Kansas
Missouri
West Virginia
Virginia
Delaware
Maryland
Kentucky
Oklahoma
Tennessee
North Carolina
Arkansas
South Carolina
Georgia
Mississippi
Alabama
Texas
Louisiana
Florida
Atlantic Ocean
Hawai'i
Scale
100 Miles
0 100 Kilometers
Alaska
Scale
500 Miles
0 500 Kilometers
Rutgers College, College Avenue Gym – New Brunswick, New Jersey On a field where the College Avenue Gym is now located, the first college football game was played in 1869. Rutgers College beat Princeton 6–4.

Quiz

1 In what year was the NCAA formed?

2 From what four sources do college athletes generate money for their schools?

3 In 2016, how much did the top five college coaches earn?

4 According the NCAA rules, how many hours in a week can a college athlete spend practicing?

5 What is the average value of an athletic scholarship?

6 How many college sports offer scholarships?

7 After finishing school, what did college soccer player Nicole Mann go on to become?

8 Which two college sports are the most profitable for their schools?

ANSWERS **1.** 1906 **2.** Ticket sales, merchandise, alumni donations, and TV stations **3.** Between \$6 million and \$9 million **4.** 20 hours **5.** Between \$10,000 and \$30,000 **6.** At least 35 **7.** An astronaut **8.** Football and basketball

Key Words

alumni: previous students of a particular school, college, or university

hydrotherapy: the use of water to treat injury or disease

insurance: money paid by a company or organization to cover certain types of costs, such as medical treatment

lawsuits: conflicts between two people or groups that are taken to court

merchandise: manufactured goods that are bought and sold

room and board: a place to live and food to eat

scholarships: money given to students to pay for educational expenses

stipend: a periodic payment

symptoms: signs of an illness or disease

tuition: a sum of money students pay to attend college

Index

Log on to www.av2books.com

AV² by Weigl brings you media enhanced books that support active learning. Go to www.av2books.com, and enter the special code found on page 2 of this book. You will gain access to enriched and enhanced content that supplements and complements this book. Content includes video, audio, weblinks, quizzes, a slide show, and activities.

AV² Online Navigation

Book Pages
AV² pages directly correspond to pages in the book.

Audio
Listen to sections of the book read aloud.

Video
Watch informative video clips.

Embedded Weblinks
Gain additional information for research.

Key Words
Study vocabulary, and complete a matching word activity.

Try This!
Complete activities and hands-on experiments.

Quizzes
Test your knowledge.

Slide Show
View images and captions, and prepare a presentation.

AV² was built to bridge the gap between print and digital. We encourage you to tell us what you like and what you want to see in the future.

Sign up to be an AV² Ambassador at www.av2books.com/ambassador.

Due to the dynamic nature of the Internet, some of the URLs and activities provided as part of AV² by Weigl may have changed or ceased to exist. AV² by Weigl accepts no responsibility for any such changes. All media enhanced books are regularly monitored to update addresses and sites in a timely manner. Contact AV² by Weigl at 1-866-649-3445 or av2books@weigl.com with any questions, comments, or feedback.